First published by Dog Ear Publishing
4011 Vincennes Road
Indianapolis, IN 46268
www.dogearpublishing.net

ISBN: 978-1-4575-5194-9

This book is printed on acid free paper.
Printed in the United States of America

THE LAND OF REVERSE

WHERE SLEEP IS JUST A MATTER
OF LETTING YOURSELF GO...

WRITTEN & ILLUSTRATED
BY DAVE MANOUSOS

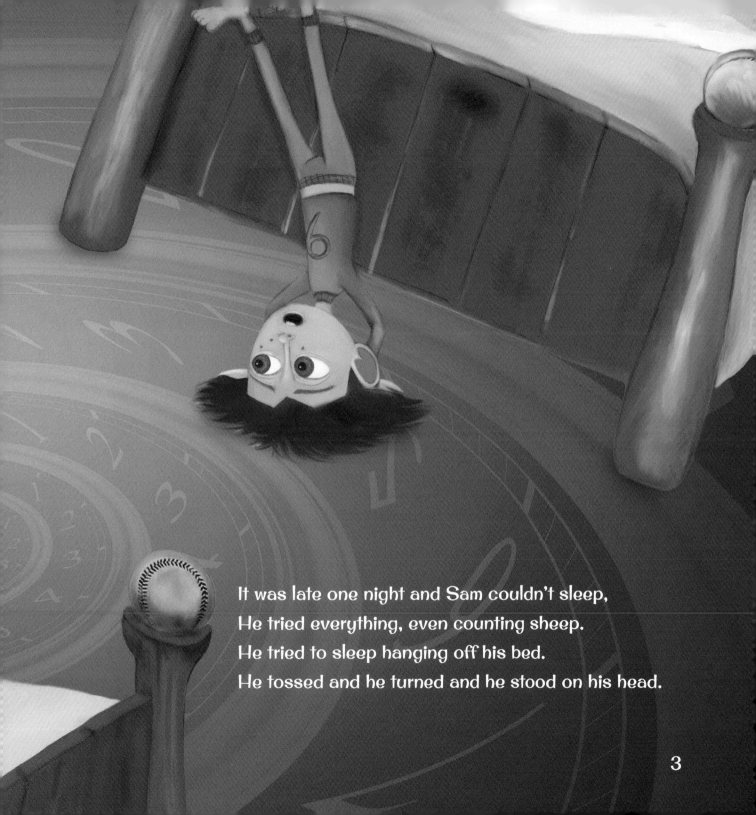

It was late one night and Sam couldn't sleep,
He tried everything, even counting sheep.
He tried to sleep hanging off his bed.
He tossed and he turned and he stood on his head.

3

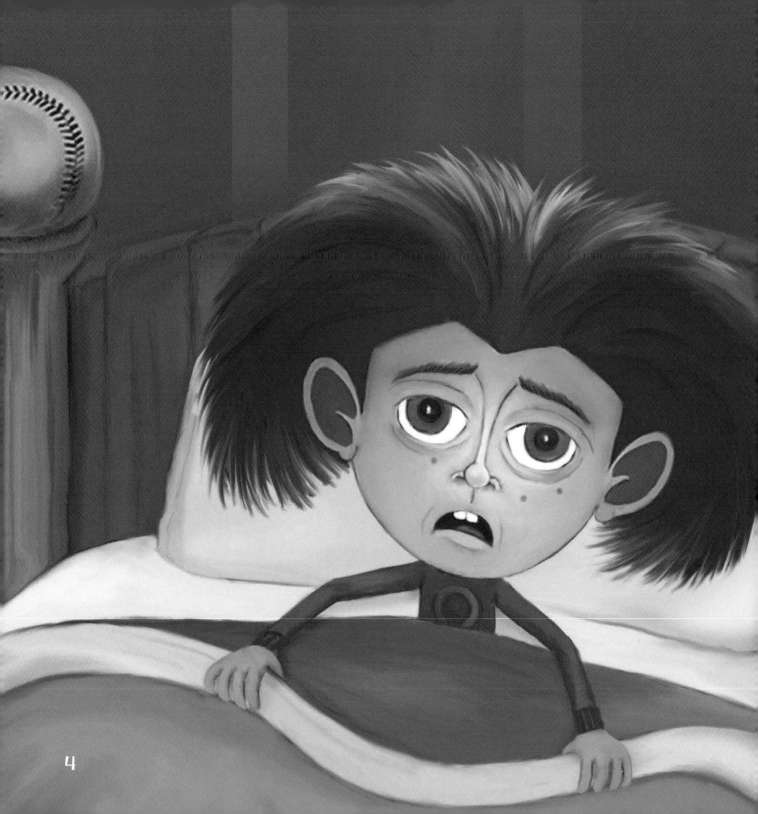

Hour after hour, Sam lay there awake.

How many tock ticks was it going to take?

Sam sat straight up with a crazy, new thought:

"I'll pretend I'm sleeping, it's the best thought I've got!"

Sam took a breath and he shut his eyes tight.
He thought ten miles left, and ten miles right.
He let his mind wander, then fell in head first,

And found he was standing in The Land of Reverse.

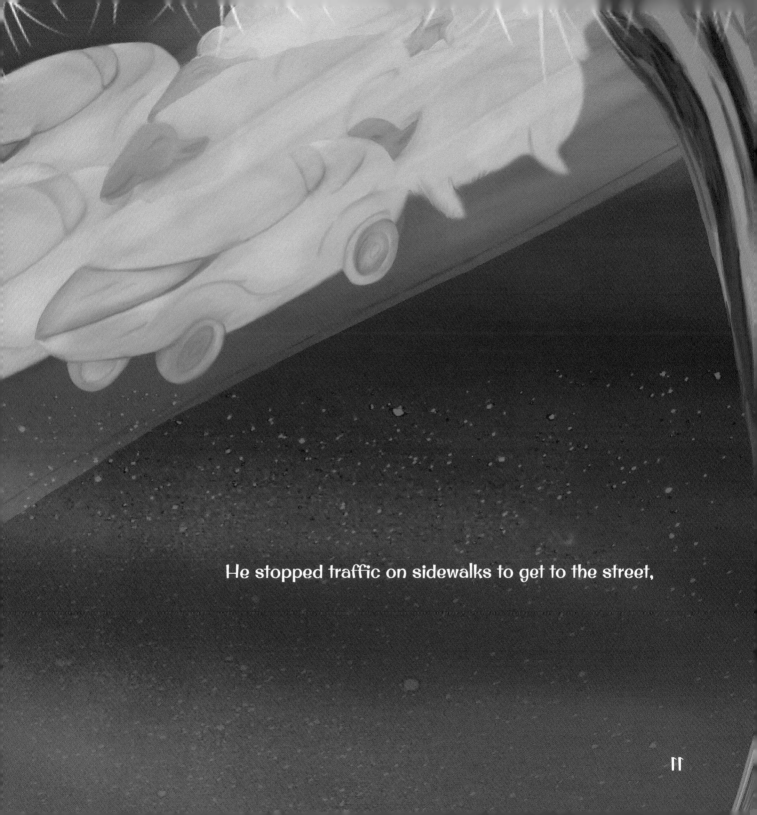

He stopped traffic on sidewalks to get to the street,

And there stood a man on his hands, not his feet.

The hand-standing man asked, "Are you lost, or found?

What you see as up, is really straight down."

"You'll see without seeing, and you'll hear things you don't.
You'll smell, taste and feel things, and then you won't.
So be off Sam, but remember this thought,
Wherever you're going, you really are not."

Although Sam was puzzled by the hand-standing man,
He took the advice, and he walked as he ran.
He ran through a wall, or was it a door?
He stood on the ceiling, and looked up at the floor.

Sam took a breath and he shut his eyes tight.
He thought ten miles left, and ten miles right.

21

Everywhere Sam saw invisible things,
Birds flying backwards without any wings,
There were fish catching people and flies eating frogs,
Mice chasing cats and cats chasing dogs.

Sam took a breath and he shut his eyes tight.
He thought ten miles left, and ten miles right.

There in the dark, Sam saw he was changing—
Even his body parts were rearranging!
His feet were his hands, and he had tiny eyes.
His head, upside down, was enormous in size!

Sam took a breath and he shut his eyes tight.
He thought ten miles left, and ten miles right.

Sam looked all around, with eyes that don't see,
Then he heard whispers that were loud as can be!
"We must feed the people, it's what animals do!
We feed people who live in the zoo."

Sam took a breath and he shut his eyes tight.
He thought ten miles left, and ten miles right.

Sam dove into land and swam underground,
While finless fish walked all around.
He swam and he swam slower than slow,
And quickly got where he wanted to go.

Sam took a breath and he shut his eyes tight.
He thought ten miles left, and ten miles right.

Going nowhere fast, Sam walked as he ran,
And there behind him stood the hand-standing man.
"You've seen many things without seeing them yet.
You've gone without going, pardon me, have we met?"

Sam took a breath and he shut his eyes tight.
He thought ten miles left, and ten miles right.

Slipping and sliding up a trunk of a tree,
Sam decided where he wanted to be.

With backward thoughts filling his head.
He found himself lying in bed.

Eyes wide open with a smile on his face,
Sam couldn't wait to go back to that place.
No tossing, no turning, no counting sheep,
He found a new way of going to sleep.

Sam took a breath and he shut his eyes tight.
He thought ten miles left, and ten miles right.

CPSIA information can be obtained at www.ICGtesting.com
Printed in the USA
LVIW01n2248171017
552824LV00004B/15